the **Fairly OddParents**!
NICKELODEON

UP ALL NIGHT

by Kim Ostrow
illustrated by
Zina Saunders

Ready-to-Read

Simon Spotlight/Nickelodeon
New York   London   Toronto   Sydney   Singapore

Butch Hartman (signature)

Based on the TV series *The Fairly OddParents*®
created by Butch Hartman as seen on Nickelodeon®

SIMON SPOTLIGHT

An imprint of Simon & Schuster Children's Publishing Division
1230 Avenue of the Americas, New York, New York 10020

Manufactured in the United States of America

First Edition
2 4 6 8 10 9 7 5 3 1

Library of Congress Cataloging-in-Publication Data
Ostrow, Kim.
Up all night / by Kim Ostrow.-- 1st ed.
p. cm. -- (Ready-to-read ; #1)
"Based on the TV show The Fairly OddParents® created by
Butch Hartman as seen on Nickelodeon."
Summary: Timmy's fairy godparents grant his wish to abolish bedtime,
but he changes his mind after dealing with Vicky, the tyrannical babysitter.
ISBN 0-689-86320-9
[1. Bedtime--Fiction. 2. Wishes--Fiction. 3. Fairies--Fiction. 4.
Babysitters--Fiction.] I. Title. II. Series.
PZ7.O8545Up 2004
[E]--dc21
2003002378

It was bedtime for Timmy Turner.
He propped himself up on his pillow
and crossed his arms.
"Going to sleep is no fun,"
Timmy complained.

Timmy thought of all
the neat things he could do
if he didn't have to sleep.
"Sleep is a very important part
of your day, Timmy," Cosmo said.

"Cosmo is right, Timmy,"
Wanda agreed. "I need my sleep.
Otherwise I can't stay awake
to grant wishes."

"Well I would rather stay up
all night long," Timmy replied.
"I wish there was no bedtime at all!"

Cosmo and Wanda made
Timmy's wish come true.
"Life just got a whole lot better,"
Timmy said, changing out of
his pajamas and tossing them
under the bed.

Just then Timmy's parents
walked into his room.
"We are off to an all-night
card game," Timmy's father declared.
"We should be back tomorrow night,
dear," said Timmy's mother.
"Vicky will be here any minute
to baby-sit."

Before Timmy could say a word
the doorbell rang. His parents let
Vicky in and said good-bye.

"Hey, Twerp. Do you know what time it is?" Vicky asked.

"No," Timmy replied.

"Time to do whatever I say," said Vicky with a wicked grin.

"I hope you know there are some
new rules around here," Timmy said.
"I can stay up as late as I want and
do whatever I want."

"Of course you can
stay up as late as you
want," said Vicky.
"But you will do
whatever **I** want!"

"Welcome to baby-sitting boot camp!"
shouted Vicky as she dragged
a huge trunk into the house.

"First, shine all three hundred
pairs of my shoes," said Vicky.
"But that could take all night!"
cried Timmy.

"Well it's a good thing you do not
have a bedtime," Vicky said.
Timmy sighed heavily and
started shining the shoes.

"Do not forget to use polish!"

Vicky shouted from the other room.

"You want polish? I will show you

polish," muttered Timmy as he spit

all over her shoes.

A few hours later Timmy was finished. "I am glad I do not have to go to sleep," he told Cosmo and Wanda. "I still have all night to do whatever I want."

As soon as he got to his bedroom
Vicky threw open the door and
stormed into his room.

"I am hungry," Vicky announced.

"Go downstairs and make me a pizza."

Timmy said no.

"Okay then, I will make a big mess in the kitchen and tell your parents you did it."

Timmy headed to the kitchen and
began fixing Vicky a pizza.
Cosmo and Wanda were trying hard
not to fall asleep. But just watching
Timmy was tiring!

When he was done Timmy yawned
and said, "Good thing I still have
all night to do whatever I want."

"Good eats, kid," said Vicky,
licking her fingers. "Now I have
more energy to boss you around—
get back to work!"

Vicky made Timmy do her math,
science, and history homework.
His eyes were feeling very heavy.
But Vicky was still wide awake!

Next Vicky pulled out a pink dress
and handed it to Timmy.

"Time to fix my dress!" she said.

"No way," he said. "I am not wearing
a dress again."

But Timmy was too tired to fight.

"This is silly," muttered Timmy.

"I wish I did not have to

wear these clothes."

Although they were very tired,

Cosmo and Wanda made Timmy's

wish come true. POOF!

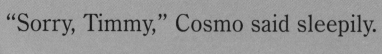

"Sorry, Timmy," Cosmo said sleepily.

"Just doing our job."

When Vicky turned around and saw

Timmy in his underwear

she fell on the floor laughing.

Timmy ran to his room.

While Timmy put on his pajamas
his fairy godparents popped into
their fishbowl.

"Let's just close our eyes
for a minute," Wanda suggested.

"Good idea . . . zzzzz," Cosmo replied.

Meanwhile Timmy was having the
worst night of his life.

"I wish my bedtime was
right now!" he yelled.

Nothing happened. He repeated his wish.

"Oh, no!" Timmy shouted.

"Cosmo and Wanda are sound asleep!"

Then Vicky burst into his room again.

"This room is too clean!" she said.

Vicky opened Timmy's closet and threw

all of his clothes on the floor.

Then she dumped out his toy box.

Finally she grabbed the fishbowl

and emptied it on Timmy's bed.

Cosmo and Wanda hit the bed and
woke up—well, Wanda did anyway.
"Five more minutes, Mom!" said Cosmo.
"Oh, wake up, Cosmo. Timmy needs us!"
said Wanda. "Okay, Timmy—make a wish."
"I wish it was bedtime!" said Timmy.

Timmy was all tucked in with his
pink hat on the pillow beside him.
"It sure feels good to be in bed,"
he said.

"Oh, Timmy!" said Vicky with a huge
pair of scissors in her hand.

"Time for a haircut!"

Timmy opened one eye and said,
"And I wish Vicky would fall asleep
until my parents come home!"

POOF!

Good night!